I Don't Like It!

RUTH BROWN

E. P. DUTTON ◆ NEW YORK

"I don't like it," the little doll sighed.
"Everything's changed since that puppy came.
My little girl plays with him all the time and
leaves me inside. I don't like it!"

"What do you think?" the doll asked the other toys. "Do you like it?"
Teddy raised his sleepy head. "I don't mind it," he said with a yawn.

"When she plays with the puppy, I have more time to rest. Now I can snooze and dream all day. I like it!"

"I might have known," said the doll. "What
about you, Jack-in-the-Box? Don't you mind it?"

"Not at all," said Jack. "Strange as it seems, I love to sit still. Jumping up and down makes my head ache. And I hate being shut in that box. When the girl is out with the puppy, I can relax. I like it!"

"Well, the mice aren't like you. I'm sure they
don't want to be left alone."
The doll knocked on the door of the mouse-
house. "Hello! Tell me—do *you* like it?"

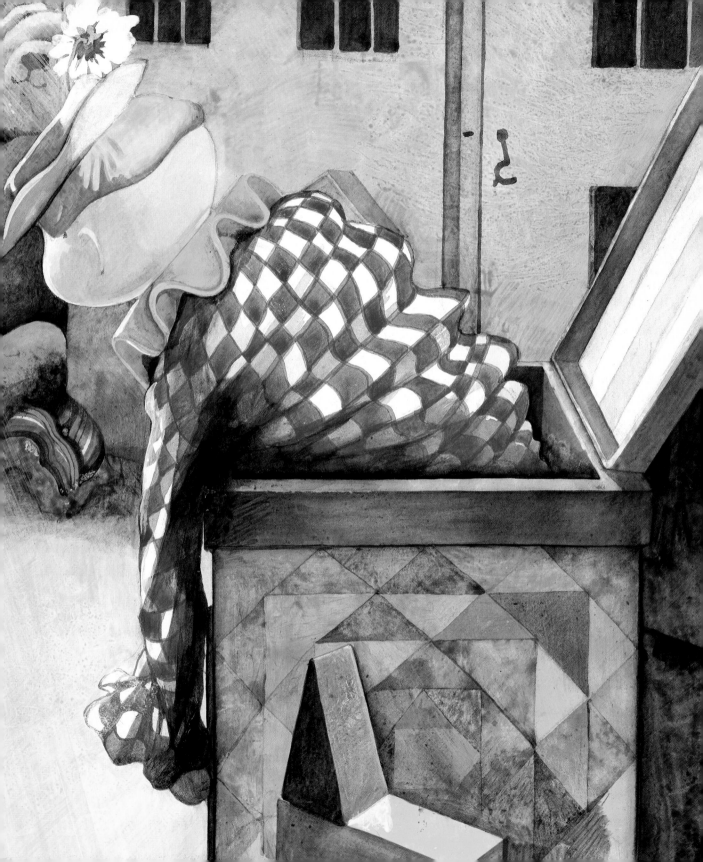

A tiny gray mouse stepped through the door.
"When the girl goes off to play, we have more
time to clean and polish our house. We like it!"

"If she had a kitten, would you like that?" sniffed the doll.
But the mouse had already gone back to her sweeping.

"I'm the only one who wants to have fun," said the little doll sadly. But she wasn't the only one.

A few minutes later, someone came down the hall. And that someone wanted to play too!

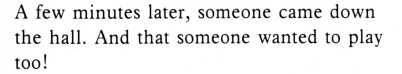

At bedtime, the little girl couldn't find her
doll. "It's lost!" she sobbed. "I want it!"
"Don't cry, dear," said her mother. "It must
be nearby. We'll find it. . . . Oh, Puppy, come
out from there."

And he did.
"Look! Puppy's found your doll," the girl's
mother said. "You'd think he knew it was there
all along." She turned off the light. "Can you
go to sleep now?"

But the little girl didn't answer.
She was already asleep.
The doll snuggled closer to the girl,
smiled, and thought, "That's more
like it!"